***Orville Rudemeyer Pygenski has a great idea
for a new club. . . .***

"ORVIE! I've got to get in the bathroom. It's an emergency."

"It's not locked, Chloe, come on in," I said.

Chloe slowly opened the door. She was surprised to find me
fully dressed sitting in the bathtub.

"What are you doing?"

"Thinking," I said. "You should try it sometime."

"You're cute. Real cute. Would you mind getting out of
here now?"

I got up and walked out. It was always fun to surprise
Chloe. As I passed through her room, I noticed she had a pamphlet from the 4-H Club on her bed.

Club . . . hmmmm, I thought. That's IT!

I could start an I Hate My Name Club.

ALSO BY SUZY KLINE

ORP

SUZY KLINE

PUFFIN BOOKS

Special appreciation for the
Drama Players at Southwest School and
Torringford School in Torrington, Connecticut,
who put on productions of ORP. Bravo!

Interior artwork by Christy Hale

PUFFIN BOOKS
Published by the Penguin Group
Penguin Putnam Books for Young Readers,
345 Hudson Street, New York, New York 10014, U.S.A.
Penguin Books Ltd, 27 Wrights Lane, London W8 5TZ, England
Penguin Books Australia Ltd, Ringwood, Victoria, Australia
Penguin Books Canada Ltd, 10 Alcorn Avenue, Toronto, Ontario, Canada M4V 3B2
Penguin Books (N.Z.) Ltd, 182-190 Wairau Road, Auckland 10, New Zealand

Penguin Books Ltd, Registered Offices: Harmondsworth, Middlesex, England

First published in the United States by G. P. Putnam's Sons,
a division of The Putnam & Grosset Group, 1989
Published by Puffin Books,
a member of Penguin Putnam Books for Young Readers, 1999

1 3 5 7 9 10 8 6 4 2

THE LIBRARY OF CONGRESS HAS CATALOGED THE G. P. PUTNAM'S SONS EDITION AS FOLLOWS:
Kline, Suzy. ORP / Suzy Kline.
p. cm. Summary: Orville Rudemeyer Pygenski, Jr.'s, decision to form an
"I Hate My Name Club" has some surprising results.
ISBN 0-399-21639-1 (hc.)
[1. Names, Personal—Fiction. 2. Clubs—Fiction. 3. Humorous stories.] I. Title.
PZ7.K67970r 1989 [Fic]—dc19 88-29911 CIP AC

This edition ISBN 0-698-11780-8

Printed in the United States of America

For my sister Nancie with love

Contents

ORP

1

Bathtub Brainstorm

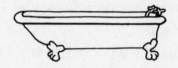

"ORVIE!" MOM HOLLERED INTO THE bathroom. "You've been in there an hour now!"

Of course I was. I get my best ideas when I'm sitting in the tub.

Today, I put my feet on the hot and cold faucet handles and leaned back. The window was wide open so I could catch a breeze—when there was one. It had to be the hottest, muggiest day in

Connecticut. And with no air-conditioning, it was murder!

I was working on a list of things I hate.

Mrs. Lewis, who runs an enrichment activity room at school, asked me to do some brainstorming over the summer. She wants me to come to school in the fall with a good idea for a project.

She suggested I make a list of things I love to do. I said I didn't feel like it. That's when she got miffed. "Make a list of things you hate, then. THAT might help."

So that's what I was doing in my think tank. I looked over my last nine entries:

    30. hot, muggy weather
    31. no milk in the fridge
    32. making my bed
    33. poverty

Mom said I didn't need to get a regular allowance this summer. She said I could earn money by doing chores.

    34. chores

I knew I was going to be poor all summer.

    35. when Ralph throws up

Ralph is my dog. I've had him for ten years. Mom and Dad gave him to me for my first birthday. Nowadays he loves to eat desserts—Mom's brownies, lemon merangue pie, butterscotch pudding, anything that's sweet! And then he throws up all over the place. Once he threw up over my bumblebee collection. If you've ever seen bumblebees coated with barf, it's a real gross out.

36. pimentoes

Mom always puts those red slimy things in her potato salad. I tell her not to, but she says they are packed with flavor and add zest to a salad. I usually manage to pick the pimentoes out but every now and then I miss one. Swallowing one of those things is a killer.

37. drying the dishes

It's not that I mind drying the dishes so much, it's just that every time I do, Mom gives me a lecture on how to use wrist movements with the dish towel so that I can add extra sparkle to the glasses.

38. Derrick's stinginess

Derrick is my best friend. Sort of. He's just so tight with his money. He never loans me a dime. And when we play Monopoly, he always gets to be banker. He's probably the only guy in the world who knows how much money is in a new Monopoly set—$15,140.00.

Right now I was on the thirty-ninth thing I hated. Mrs. Lewis said when you're brainstorming, the best idea is usually the last one.

"ORVIE! GET OUT OF THAT BATHROOM!"

That was my sister, Chloe, banging on the door.

I put the breadboard that I was balancing over the edges of the tub on the bathroom floor. "All right! All right, I'm getting out," I said, adding my sister's name to the list.

Chloe is going to be in fifth grade next year. She loves to write. I sure don't. Writing was number thirteen on my hate list. Chloe is doing a project with Mrs. Lewis too, but it's a novel. It has a stupid name like *Marsha's First Love*. She always bugs me with dumb questions about names for characters and where kids go on dates. I don't know! I've never gone on one. Derrick's been talking about it, though. He says we should go on at least one date this summer before seventh grade. He said we're probably the only guys at Cornell Middle School who haven't gone out with a girl. I told him to forget it. I wasn't going to. Not in a billion years. Make that a quintillion.

"ORVILLE RUDEMEYER PYGENSKI, Jr.!" Mom hollered again from the living room.

I had my final entry. Number forty-one. I

printed it neatly in big letters and underlined it. My name. I hated it more than anything. I'll never forget being the only kid in first grade who could not spell his name. Course, my teacher couldn't spell it either. She always had to look it up in the roll book.

By the time I got to second grade, I got smart. I used my initials O, R, and P and made the name Orp. All the kids at school call me that. Except Chloe. She copies Mom and calls me Orvie. That's worse than Orville.

"ORVIE!"

Now both Mom and Chloe were shouting. I figured I better hustle out of the bathroom.

I draped a faded bath towel around my waist and walked into the living room dripping a little bit of water on the floor.

"Have you no morals?" Chloe said in disgust.

"Feast your eyes upon a real man," I smiled.

"Where?" Chloe remarked. "Ralph's outside."

"Nevermind, idiot. What do you want, Mom?"

"I need some help around here. Lift this corner of the couch for me so I can move it."

"How come you want to rearrange furniture on a hot day like today? Have mercy, Mom. It's ninety degrees."

"I know, I know. But, the Washburns are coming tomorrow and I want this living room to look more spacious."

"Who are the Washburns?" I asked.

"Don't you remember?"

"No."

"They visited us when you were two."

Geez, I thought. How does Mom expect me to remember company at that age?

"Hilda Washburn was my best friend in high school. She and her husband, Melvin, and daughter, Jennifer, will be here tomorrow from Ohio."

I didn't like the name Hilda or Melvin either. "How long are they staying?"

"A month."

"A MONTH?" I couldn't believe it. My home was being invaded by strangers!

"They plan to take side trips so actually our house will be more like a base."

An army base, I thought. Now there would be all kinds of rules in our house—like not walking around in a towel. What kind of a life would that be? I decided to pursue the matter. "Where are they sleeping?"

"We can discuss that later."

I knew what Mom was saying. Somebody

would be sleeping in *my* bed. I didn't like this Washburn visit at all.

"Hurry up and get dressed, Orvie. I need you to help me with this couch."

"All right," I grumbled.

When I returned, Mom started counting. "Ready? One, two . . . three—lift!"

I lifted my corner. "Where are we taking this?" I said, gasping for air.

"By the windows . . . *Auuuugh!*" Mom shrieked. We both dropped the couch.

"What's the matter, Mom?"

"My God in Heaven!" she shouted. "I stepped on a sewing needle!" Mom showed me the bottom of her foot. I couldn't see anything.

"It's . . . it's in my foot!" Mom cried. "The needle went right up."

"I'll get the tweezers," I said.

"Nevermind," Mom cried. "It's too far up."

"You sure?"

"Sure, I'm sure. Call your dad."

I was getting nervous. But Mom was worse. "Hurry up! If that needle gets into my bloodstream, it will be destined for my heart!"

I think Mom was overreacting, but as I began dialing my dad's business number, I had a picture of that needle floating like a raft through my mother's blood vessels. That was when Chloe came running in. She had a pen over one ear. "What's happening?"

"Mom stepped on a needle. We're going to the emergency room. Go get her slippers. She needs to wear floppy shoes."

"Sounds like a possible plot. Maybe I can use it."

"Get the slippers!" I shouted.

"Excuse me?" the voice on the phone said.

"I'm sorry, I wasn't talking to you. May I have extension 382?"

"One moment, please."

Dad got home in five minutes. We would have left right away, but no one could find Mom's slippers. I finally ran outside and looked in Ralph's doghouse. They were there. Half-chewed.

"Where have those been?" Mom said making a face.

"In Ralph's mouth. Do you think you spilled some dessert on them?" I couldn't figure out why Ralph was eating them.

"I'm dying and you're asking me about dessert!"

"Just go barefooted, Mom."

"I'd rather die than show these hairy toes."

All three of us looked at Mom's toes. There were clumps of black hair on them. I didn't realize women got hair there.

"What if I bumped into someone I knew?" Mom continued. "Just look at my feet. I didn't have time to shave."

It was news to me that women shaved their toes. Obviously Mom did. "Mom," I said, "this is not the time for high fashion. Why don't you just slip these on?"

Mom grabbed her half-chewed slippers and put them on.

The lady at the desk in the emergency room asked my mother about her insurance plan. "Oh, it's with my husband's business."

Dad took over from there.

"Your name, please?" the lady continued.

"Orville Rudemeyer Pygenski, Sr."

"Spell it slowly, please," she smirked.

Here was an emergency situation and Mom had to wait around because of a dumb name. I could tell Dad wasn't too happy with the idea.

"O . . . r . . . v . . ."

"Is that V as in victory or B as in banana?"

"V as in virus," Dad said, making a frown.

I figured that needle probably was in Mom's

bloodstream by now. I decided to sit down next to her. Chloe was stroking her arm. "You'll be fine, Mom. That's what you always tell us," she said.

"Yes, dear. I must get a hold of myself." She reached for a book on the table and set it on her lap. "After all, I'm forty years old now. I must be mature about this whole thing."

With that, she picked up the book and started reading. Chloe gestured for me to look at the book cover. It said, *Bozo's Trip to the Zoo*. It was hard not to laugh. Mom kept turning the pages of that book and looking at the pictures.

Dad was still spelling our name at the front desk.

"Is that P as in pillow or B as in banana?"

I could tell Dad was really getting angry because he took his jacket off and rolled up his sleeves. "Look, I'll spell the rest for you: P as in piranha, Y as in yellow fever, G as in garter snake, E as in ether, N as in needle . . ."

That was when Mom started to cry. The word needle was too much for her.

Finally, Dad's "Operation Spelldown" was over and Mom got called to the X-ray room.

Dr. Goldberg showed us the slides as soon as they were developed. I thought they looked neat. The needle in Mom's heel reminded me of a rocket about to be launched at Cape Canaveral.

"It's either going to be real easy or . . ."

Mom covered her eyes.

"Let's go Mrs. Py—"

"genski," I helped.

Mom was lucky. The needle came out easy. Dr. Goldberg gave her foot Novocain so she didn't feel anything. He offered her the needle as a souvenir, but she said no thanks.

"I'll take it," I said. "I collect everything."

2

The "I Hate My Name Club"

THE WHOLE MORNING'S EPISODE AT THE emergency room made me realize how much I hate my name. The problem was, what could I do about it?

When we got back from the hospital I decided to return to my think tank. As I sat in the tub, I thought about different solutions. I could save up money and get a lawyer to change my name when I was eighteen. But that was seven years away.

I could run away from home and then turn up in another city with a new name . . . like Joe Smith. But I kind of liked living at my house, even if I had to deal with the Washburns. So, scratch that idea, I thought.

"ORVIE! I've got to get in the bathroom. It's an emergency!"

"It's not locked, Chloe, come on in," I said.

Chloe slowly opened the door. She was surprised to find me fully dressed sitting in the bathtub.

"What are you doing?"

"Thinking," I said. "You should try it sometime."

"You're cute. Real cute. Would you mind getting out of here now?"

I got up and walked out. It was always fun to surprise Chloe. As I passed through her room, I noticed she had a pamphlet from the 4-H Club on her bed.

Club . . . hmmmm, I thought. That's IT!

I could start an I Hate My Name Club.

As I sat down on Chloe's bed, I started to think

of what it might be like. I'd have to have a secretary, of course. There would be lots of advertising to do just to get started.

Secretary. Who could I get in the summer who liked to write and had a rotten name?

Just then I heard a gargling noise from the bathroom.

CHLOE!

I got up and tapped lightly on the bathroom door. "Chloe, still in there?"

"Yes, why?"

"How would you like to be . . . a secretary of an important club?"

Chloe opened the door a crack. "What important club?"

"The I Hate My Name Club. Aren't you tired of your name—Chloe Urath Rudemeyer Pygenski?"

"Kind of," she said. "Actually, I have been using a pen name when I write my novel—Jane Ear."

I decided not to laugh. It wasn't in the best interests of our club.

"What would an I Hate My Name Club do?"

"We could do important things. Not tease other kids with unusual names, promise not to pass on our unusual names to our own children . . ."

Actually, I was never planning on getting married, but I thought that reason made sense.

"How do you get members?" Chloe continued her questioning.

"That's where you come in. I'll give you fifty index cards and you could type information on them about our club."

"Seems like a lot of work." Chloe dried her hands on a towel.

"I'd put the cards up all over town, and then we'd just wait and see who contacted us."

The door opened wide. Chloe flashed her teeth at me. They smelled like peppermint. "Not interested," she said.

I decided to appeal to her interest in writing. "Nice way to meet new people. Might be some good characters for future stories."

"I already have two—Marsha and Heathcliff." Chloe sat down and started typing at her desk.

"Look," I said, shoving her out of her chair and removing the piece of paper that was in the typewriter. "You take an index card like this, insert it, and type this."

After two minutes, I showed her the card.

```
HATE YOUR NAME???

Join the I HATE MY NAME Club

Write to: ORP, President
          134 Laurington Avenue

Hartford, CT  06104

(Kids only 8-12 years)
```

"Isn't that an eye-grabber?"

Chloe took the card and examined it. "Not particularly," she said, handing the card back to me. Then she pushed me off the chair, reinserted her paper and continued typing.

I tried one more time.

"You might just need some new ideas for plots."

"I told you, Orp, I already have one."

"Yeah, but will you have one for your next novel, and the next?" I tried to be dramatic.

"Huh?"

I figured I had her now. "Don't you know what WRITER'S BLOCK is?"

"Writer's block?"

"Yeah."

"Never heard of it. Is that where writers live?"

"Funny. Listen, smartie, writer's block is like a disease. If you get it, you can't think of one thing to write. You sit in your chair and have a blank mind."

"Really?"

"Really."

It was quiet for the next minute.

"What's the matter?" I asked.

"My mind just went blank."

I didn't say anything. I just smiled.

"Well," Chloe finally said, "all right, but I'm just typing twenty-five cards and I'm charging you five cents each. Labor. I don't care if I'm the secretary of your club, someone has to pay me for my services."

"But this is a volunteer club. Nobody makes a profit."

"I do. I have to buy my own typing paper."

I needed her. And I was desperate. "Okay, five cents a card."

"Deal."

"Let me know when you're finished. I want to get started with this advertising campaign as soon as possible."

"I'll make it a rush job."

"Good."

Things were definitely looking up. I was now president of a real club at the age of eleven. I had my own secretary and advertising campaign. All I needed was a vice president, treasurer, and some members.

3

Vivian Goes on a Date

THE NEXT DAY WAS HOTTER. WE ONLY have one fan in our house and Ralph knocked it over. Dad said he'd fix it but he's never gotten to it. Actually there are a lot of things he hasn't gotten to, like our broken TV knob and oven timer.

In the meantime whenever Mom has to cook, we all suffer.

Today Mom was baking beans.

"Do you have to?" I pleaded.

"I want the Washburns to have a real New England home-cooked meal when they arrive tonight," Mom said hobbling over to the sink. I think she felt some pain in her foot now.

"The beans aren't the ONLY thing baking in this house, Mom," I complained.

"Funny, Orvie," she said, as she dropped a cup of raisins in a bowl of batter. "Here, take this money and go to the movies with Chloe. I don't need any more smart comments today. I have too much to do."

"I'll accept this bribe for three reasons, Mom," I said. "One, the movie theater is air-conditioned and this house is like a torture chamber. Two, I already called Derrick and he's not home. And three, I never refuse money."

"I see," Mom replied.

I was getting pretty good at listing things. "Come on Chloe!" I yelled.

As we were walking down the street, Chloe handed me a pile of cards. "Finished," she said.

I flipped through them. They looked pretty good, but I found one error. "You typed 'Blub' instead of 'Club.' See?"

"So, no one's perfect."

"Ah . . . but there's me," I grinned.

"Just give me my money," Chloe said.

"I'll pay you a dollar twenty, not a dollar twenty-five."

"Cheapskate," she said taking the change.

I stuffed the cards in my hip pocket. Was I getting to be like Derrick?

It was good to know we could start the advertising campaign. We thought about putting one up in the movie lobby, but I didn't have any tape.

"Want to use a thumbtack?" Chloe said.

"Sure, but where do we get one?"

"Easy," Chloe replied, lifting her foot. There was a thumbtack in the sole of her shoe.

"Clever," I said. "Why don't we tack it on the wall next to the Coke machine?"

"Yeah."

Our first official notice, I thought.

We took a step back and admired it.

When the two lighters were talking to each other on the screen about not flicking Bics in the theater, Chloe decided to get a drink. "Don't take long," I whispered. "The movie's about to start."

I watched Chloe scoot through the aisle. She had stuffed her long red hair in her baseball cap. What a nut, I thought. Just then I noticed two kids sitting down three rows in front of me. It was Derrick Jones and Ellen Fairchild. So THAT'S why Derrick wasn't home when I called. What an operator! He actually asked Ellen Fairchild for a date to the movies. I didn't believe it. He had been talking about doing it all year. Guess he was waiting for the summer Wednesday matinees when admission is half-price. I noticed he had his arm halfway around the back of her chair.

"That drinking fountain was gross. Someone left a wad of gum in it," Chloe said as she sat down next to me.

Oh, geez, I thought. Here I am at the movies with my sister, and Derrick has to be in the same theater with a date.

I moved two seats over. I wasn't sitting next to Chloe now.

"Is that Derrick and Ellen Fairchild in front of us?"

"Shhh!" I said. "Keep your voice down. I don't want them to see us."

"He's got his arm around her!" Chloe's voice was louder now.

All I could think about was murdering my sister. She never did learn to whisper. Never.

Then I thought about something else. What if Derrick or Ellen saw that notice next to the Coke

32

machine? I wasn't so sure I wanted them to know about it. I wanted to have an I Hate My Name Club, but I guess I wanted it to be secret for a while.

"Chloe," I whispered across the two empty seats, "go out and get that notice we put up. I don't want people around here to know about it."

"Huh?"

"I mean, let's get new blood. Let's just put the notices up in downtown Hartford. I'd like to meet new people, okay?"

"You mean you don't want Derrick and Ellen to know about it?" Chloe had a way of getting to the point.

"Yeah."

"Why not? Don't you like them?"

"Sure, but they might . . ."

"Shhh!" a lady from the aisle behind us said.

I whispered even softer ". . . they might laugh or something."

"Why? This is a serious club. Aren't you serious?"

Suddenly I was embarrassed. Chloe was right. I was president of something important. I was ashamed of myself. "You're right!" I said.

I slouched back down in my chair and watched

the movie. I was dreading bumping into Derrick and Ellen after the movie, but there was no avoiding it.

Derrick spotted us as soon as the lights came on. "Hey, Orp! Who's your girlfriend?"

I wanted to run out of the theater, but I didn't. I also wanted to strangle Derrick, but I didn't. "Funny. I HAD to bring my sister."

"I HAD to come with him," Chloe said pointing at me.

Ellen just smiled. She had her long brown hair pulled back with wooden barrettes. She was without a doubt the prettiest girl in our sixth-grade class.

As we walked into the lobby, Derrick asked Ellen if she wanted a Coke.

"Yes, thank you."

I was secretly hoping she would have said no. As Derrick stood in front of the machine, I wondered if he would notice the card.

"See our advertisement?" Chloe blurted out.

Oh, brother, I thought.

"You mean this?" Derrick pointed to the card on the wall and read it. "No kidding. An I Hate My Name Club."

Derrick wasn't laughing. And he didn't make any jokes. Ellen didn't either.

"Can I join, Orp?"

I was stunned. Shocked. Derrick Jones wanted to be in the club?

"Why? There's nothing wrong with your name."

"Yeah? You don't know my FULL name."

"What is it?" I asked.

"Let's get our Cokes at Ortman's Ice Cream Shop. I'll tell you there. It's more private. What I am about to tell you is *very* confidential."

We took a table by the window and behind a huge rubber plant. "Four Cokes," Derrick told the waitress. Then he leaned over and whispered, "You guys don't know that I have a middle name."

"You told me you didn't have one," I said.

"I lied." Derrick shrugged.

"What is it?" we all asked.

"Promise you'll keep it a secret?"

"Promise," we said.

"Can I be treasurer, if I tell you?"

"What is it?" Ellen asked again.

Derrick leaned over the table and whispered, "Vivian."

"VIVIAN?" we repeated.

"It's a name for men in England. My dad was born there."

Nobody said a word. We just leaned back in our chairs.

"That's why I never told anyone. In the United States, I've got a girl's name! I'm Derrick Vivian Jones!"

"You can be treasurer," I said.

"Can I join too?" Ellen asked.

"Do you have a middle name you hate?" I said. "Ellen Fairchild is a nice name."

"No. But, I believe in your cause."

I thought about it. "What do you think?" I asked Chloe and Derrick.

"Why not? She could be vice president," Chloe suggested.

"Yeah," Derrick added.

"Raise your right hand," I said forcefully to both of them. I knew I would never put our club down again. It was a going-concern now. "Do you swear never to tease a kid with a dumb name?"

Derrick and Ellen raised their hands. "I swear."

"Do you swear never to name your kid after your relative if he has a rotten name?"

"I swear."

"Do you promise to be kind to kids with terrible names?"

"I promise."

"You're in the club then."

"Let's make a Coke toast," I announced. "To the officers of the I Hate My Name Club!"

We clicked our glasses. I don't think I ever felt as great as I did then. We made plans to meet the next day to put up the rest of the cards all over town.

4

The First Member

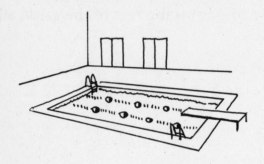

"**H**ILDA!" MOM SCREAMED AS SHE opened the door.

"Margie!" Mrs. Washburn screamed back.

I closed the hallway door. We had only been home from the movies an hour, and the Washburns were here already.

"What's a good name for a boy?" Chloe asked me from her typewriter.

"What?"

"I want something different for my story."

Chloe was asking me about names again. "How about Joe, or Bob?"

"No I need something new."

I peeked through a crack at the door and saw Mr. Washburn sitting on a kitchen chair. He was asking Mom if we had a fan.

"Our dog knocked it over, Melvin. I'm sorry."

"Melvin," I said. I felt sorry for the guy.

"Thanks!" Chloe went on typing.

"For what?"

"The name Melvin. I like it."

Geez, I thought. Chloe could be a real turkey. Then I spied someone else in the kitchen. She had braces and her hair was real short. She reminded me of some ice skater on TV. I couldn't think of her name, though.

"Can you think of a good one for a girl, now?" Chloe asked.

"Dorothy! That's it," I said. She did remind me of Dorothy Hamill.

"Thanks."

I turned around and saw Chloe typing away. I knew I would never understand my sister.

"Orville! Chloe! Come and meet the Washburns," Mom called from the kitchen.

I just remember being introduced to Jennifer Washburn.

"Hi, Jennifer," was all I could say. I kept staring at her eyes. They were like the water in our YMCA pool.

"Take her suitcase to your room, dear," Mom said. "She'll be staying there. You don't mind do you?"

I shook my head.

"I like your room," Jennifer said as she sat down on the bed. "You collect rocks?" She pointed to a box of them on my night stand.

"Last year I did. This is smoky quartz," I said, holding up one of the rocks.

"Limestone bubbles when you put vinegar on it, huh?"

"Yeah. Did you ever try it?"

"I have a science experiment book at home. I like stuff like that."

"Do you like this one?" I held up a piece of rose quartz. It sparkled in the afternoon sun shining through my window. So did Jennifer's hair. I wondered if she washed it three or four times to get it that shiny.

"It's beautiful."

"Your hair is," I blurted out. Then I looked away. I couldn't believe I said that.

40

"Huh?" she replied.

"I said some of these rocks have hair on them. My dog Ralph sits on the collection now and then."

Jennifer laughed.

I thought I got out of that blooper pretty well.

"You collect coins too?" She walked over to my desk where I had some mounted in a scrapbook.

"Couple of years ago. I collect just about everything. And make lists. That list over there is about the Olympic winners."

"What's this?" Jennifer said pointing at my bumblebee collection.

I didn't want to tell her they were encrusted with year-old barf. "Eh . . . they're a special species."

"Hmmm, curious little things."

"What do you think of New England?" I decided to change the subject.

"It's beautiful here. I think we're going to Maine next week."

Then it was quiet for a while.

"What are you interested in now?" Jennifer asked.

I debated whether or not I should tell her about the club. She seemed like an understanding person. Why not?

"I'm starting an I Hate My Name Club this summer."

"Really? You don't like your name?"

"I hate it."

"I think Orville is an interesting name. When Mom told me we were coming here, I wondered what you'd be like. I was right."

"Right?"

"I thought a person named Orville would probably be very interesting. You are. Look how many interests you have."

I never thought someone might actually like my name.

"But, I know what it's like to hate your name."

"You do?" I leaned against my window and stared at her.

"I hate my name too."

"You do?" I couldn't imagine why. Jennifer Washburn had such a nice sound.

"Do you know how many Jennifers are in my class?"

I shook my head.

"Three! I am Jennifer W. There's a Jennifer T. and a Jennifer S."

I thought about our sixth-grade class. We had two Jennifers.

"Everytime I hear Jennifer, I stop whatever I'm

42

doing. Then when I hear T. or S., I know it's not me. Sometimes, it drives me crazy!"

After a moment of silence, she added. "So, can I join your club, Orville?"

I couldn't believe it.

I had my very first member. And she had Dorothy Hamill hair, and eyes like the water in our YMCA pool.

5

Pizza and a Ferris Wheel Ride

THE NEXT MORNING, THE PHONE RANG. I took the phone into the living room since Mr. Washburn was frying bacon in the kitchen.

"Orp?" It was Derrick.

"Yeah."

"When do you want to leave for our ad campaign?"

"How about this morning. And guess what?"

"What?"

"We've got our first member."

"Already?"

"Well, it's someone who's visiting us. Jennifer Washburn."

"Her middle name is rotten like mine?"

"No."

"She believes in the cause like Ellen?"

"Yeah, and she hates her name."

"Why?"

"There are three Jennifers in her class."

"Oh. What does she look like?"

"What's THAT got to do with anything?"

"We could double-date."

"Double what?" I noticed Chloe had come into the living room with the needle-nose pliers. I knew what she wanted to do. Watch TV. "I thought you were writing a story?" I said cupping the phone.

"Just taking a break."

"Yeah, well, take it somewhere else. This is private."

"The living room isn't a private place. It belongs to everyone in the family."

Chloe could be such a pain. "Just a minute,

Derrick." I gathered up the telephone wire and took it into the bathroom. THAT was the only private place in our house. I sat down in the tub and continued the conversation.

"Derrick—you still there?"

"What do you think?"

"About what?"

"A double date. We could stop for a pizza downtown."

"You know I don't date girls."

"Just tag along. You'll like it."

"Well . . ." It didn't sound too bad. We probably would get hungry after posting all those signs around town. "Yeah . . . okay."

The Washburns and Mom had plans to visit the gun museum, so Chloe decided to go with them. It was perfect. Jennifer said she'd rather go with me then look at guns.

We met Ellen and Derrick at the bus stop. Ellen and Jennifer got along from the beginning. They even sat together on the bus. Derrick was disappointed about that.

"Want to put a card on the bus?" Ellen turned around and asked.

"Good idea," I said taking a roll of masking tape out of my pocket. It looked terrific next to the bus window.

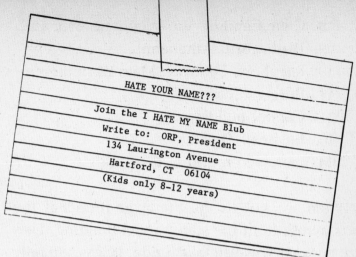

HATE YOUR NAME???

Join the I HATE MY NAME Blub
Write to: ORP, President
134 Laurington Avenue
Hartford, CT 06104
(Kids only 8-12 years)

"What's a Blub?" Derrick asked.

"Oh!" I said, "that's the card Chloe goofed on. But it was free."

"Free?" Derrick said.

"Nevermind." I took a pen out of my other pocket and changed the B to a C.

The rest of the morning we walked all over. I noted every place we taped an index card. The list included:

1. elevator of Sage Allen Department Store
2. Hartford Public Library bulletin board
3. House of Muffins
4. Mark Twain House
5. Fantasia Ice Cream Shop
6. Harriet Beecher Stowe House
7. McDonald's

When we got to the merry-go-round at the park across from the state capitol building, Derrick suggested we all take a ride. It was still only ten cents. I always thought the merry-go-round was babyish, but the girls wanted to. Jennifer chose a camel with purple reins. Ellen got on a white stallion and Derrick hopped on a rooster. The tiger I was on turned out to be one of the animals that didn't go up or down. That was embarrassing.

"Way to go, Orp!" Derrick laughed.

I was glad when the ride was over. "Let's eat. I'm starved," I said. We all walked into a pizza place and ordered a large pizza, half mushroom and half sausage. (The girls wanted mushroom, and Derrick and I wanted sausage.)

If this was a double date, it was no big deal. The girls sat on one side of the table, and Derrick and I sat on the other.

"Do you really think kids will write to you, Orp?" Jennifer asked, biting into a mushroom.

"Depends," I said. "Some kids will write. Some won't. The kids who hate their names a lot will probably make the effort. Wouldn't you?"

"My Mom would probably tell me I couldn't. She'd say you never know if those people are creep-os."

"Well, the president *is* a creep-o." Derrick laughed.

"So is the treasurer," I added.

The girls laughed.

"What if someone takes the cards down?" Ellen asked.

"That might happen. We'll just have to take that chance," I said, wiping my mouth with a napkin. I felt like I should use my napkin more often since I was eating with girls.

By the time we posted twenty-three cards, it was time to ride the 3:02 bus home. When we got off at the shopping center near our house, we noticed that there was a mini-carnival in front of Caldors Department Store.

"When did they put all this up?" Derrick asked, stepping off the bus.

"Last week. My dad said it was some kind of a promotion thing to get more people to shop."

49

Derrick looked at Ellen. "Want to take a ride on the Ferris wheel?"

"Sure!" And they ran off to get in line.

"Do you want to ride it too?"

"I never have," Jennifer said softly.

"Really? It's lots of fun." Then I wondered if I should have said that. I didn't know if I really wanted to sit *that* close to a girl or not.

"Okay."

It looked like I was.

The attendant put the handlebar over our laps. There wasn't much room to sit. Our hips were right next to each other. I tried to be casual about the whole thing. "Want to put a card on the back of our seat?"

"Good idea. Lots of kids will be riding this." Jennifer handed me some tape. She was keeping it for me in her purse.

I didn't know what to say after that.

I was glad when the thing started to move.

"We won't fall will we?" Jennifer asked.

"No." I could tell she was getting nervous.

"I really don't like heights," she said, holding the bar tightly.

When we were at the top of the Ferris wheel, it stopped for an unloading. Our seat swung back and forth a little.

50

"I'm terrified!" she suddenly yelled. And then she buried her head in my chest. I couldn't move. That Dorothy Hamill hairdo was just underneath my chin. Somehow I just put my arms around her.

Jennifer stayed buried in my arms until the ride was over.

I liked it.

I was real disappointed when the ride was over. Jennifer apologized for acting like a baby. I said it was okay. I wondered if she secretly liked being that close to me. I knew one thing—I wasn't going to ask!

I just didn't expect our advertising campaign to turn out like this.

6

Liver and Salamander

THE NEXT MORNING MR. WASHBURN DE-cided to leave for Maine early. I think he had had it with our broken fan, and fiddling with the long-nose pliers to turn the TV on. Nobody would want to stay in our house during the summer.

"Drive carefully! Enjoy the ocean," Mom said as she waved to them.

"We'll drop you a postcard. See you in a week and a half," Hilda called from the open car window.

"Good luck with your club!" Jennifer shouted.

And then Mr. Washburn peeled out.

Mom came over to me as we walked back up the porch. "What's this about a club?"

I knew I had to tell her some time. This was probably as good a time as ever.

She listened.

The more I talked the more she lowered her eyebrows. "You're *that* unhappy with your name?" she groaned.

I tried to be diplomatic, so I kind of shrugged.

"Your Uncle Rudemeyer started a pepper factory in Poland. The Pygenskis worked hard and they were good people."

"Of course they were, Mom. It's just a difficult name to say and spell. Remember Dad in the emergency room? He wasn't happy to go through that ordeal. Remember . . . Y as in yellow fever, N as in . . ."

"Don't remind me," she said, and then she walked into the kitchen.

Mom looked hurt.

She'd get over it, I thought. I decided to write a short note to my uncle in Poland, and then ask

Mom to mail it for me. That would help, maybe. I wanted to show her I still liked my relatives. I also wanted to hold meetings in my backyard. I couldn't afford to get Mom too bugged.

Two days later there were two letters in my mailbox addressed to ORP. I knew it was about the club.

I called Derrick. He called Ellen. We had a brief officers' meeting in my backyard and read the letters.

"Well, open it up, Orp," Chloe insisted. "I can't wait to find out about our first member."

"We already have our first member," I corrected her. "Jennifer will be back in a week and a half. She went to Maine with her parents. But she's very interested in our club."

"Eh hem, very interested," Derrick replied, raising his eyebrows up and down.

I gave him a jab. I knew what he was thinking.

Everyone watched me open the envelope. Slowly I read it aloud:

Dear Orp,
 I saw your sign in the 4th Avenue bus. What a great idea! I didn't know there was someone else who hated their name.
 I have ever since the kids at school have been calling me reptile.
 When's your next meeting?

                From,
              Sally Mander

"Sally Mander?" Derrick repeated. Then he cracked up. I did too.

Chloe just looked at us and stared. "I thought we weren't going to make fun of people with dumb names? Isn't that the purpose of this club?"

Derrick looked down at the grass under the picnic table.

I felt about as tall as a reptile. Chloe was right. "No more laughing," I said in a solemn voice.

"Down to business," Derrick agreed, as he put his elbows on the table. "Open the other letter."

o Dear Orp,
   It's about time there was an I HATE MY NAME club. Thanks for putting that sign on the bulletin board in the library.
   Let me know how I can o join and how much the dues are.
                    Sincerely,
                    Ignatius Liverton

o

Derrick put his hand over his mouth. I did too. We weren't going to laugh this time. But, it was hard. Liver made me sick.

"Dues?" Ellen said. "We didn't talk about that."

Derrick immediately sat up and smiled. "Yeah, well, that's why I'm here. I'm the treasurer, re-member?"

"True," Chloe replied.

"So, I'll take care of the money," Derrick added.

I could tell he was enjoying the conversation. "What do we need the money for?" I asked.

"Secretarial fees, for one," Chloe said. "And stamps, and refreshments for the meetings, and . . ."

"Okay, okay. Any suggestions how much?" I asked.

Derrick beamed, "Ten bucks for members. Of-ficers free."

We just looked at him. "How about two dollars from everyone?" I suggested.

"That's better," Ellen replied.

"Sounds fine," Chloe agreed.

Derrick just shrugged.

"It's decided then," I said. "Our dues are two

dollars." I liked being president. It seemed like we were making important decisions.

Then Derrick asked if there were any refreshments for our first meeting.

"No," I said. "We don't dare go in my kitchen. Mom is probably fuming."

I decided to explain why later.

"This meeting is adjourned," I said.

A Mailbag of Letters!

I WAS BEGINNING TO GET DISCOURAGED about our club. Four days had passed and so far we still had more officers than members. There just wasn't any more mail coming in.

That's when Derrick got his brainstorm. He placed an ad in the *Hartford Courant*. (We had a balance of six dollars. Everyone paid their dues except for Derrick.)

At first I wasn't too thrilled. "How many kids read the want ads?" I asked. I didn't think it was that great an idea.

"Haven't you ever lost a cat, or a dog and placed an ad?" Derrick said.

". . . maybe, but I think it's a lost cause."

"Don't be a pessimist, Orp. Think of Monopoly! You know how it hurts to buy a hotel for Boardwalk. But when someone lands on it—hey! You're in 'Buck City'!"

I didn't say anything. I just knew it was always easy for Derrick to spend money when it was someone else's.

In two days, however, Derrick's idea turned out to be a real winner. We got twenty-two responses! Chloe kept a record of all their names and addresses:

1. Phineas Hurdle
2. Seymour Clear
3. Heidi Ho
4. Euripides Schwartz
5. Tyrus String
6. Pepper Mintz
7. Kitty Kaat
8. Elmer Semple
9. Atlas Webster

10. Rufus Huckaby
11. Anne Chovey
12. Candy Kane
13. Percival Northrup
14. Marion Miller
15. Ida Pill
16. Waldo Whimper
17. Quigley Watson
18. Druella Smith
19. Esmeralda Walsh
20. Geronimo Jones
21. Daisy Busch
22. Robin Banks

"Wow! What a list," Derrick replied. "And there is even a Jones in the bunch like me! But look at his first name—Geronimo. I bet no one teases that guy."

"I wonder what's so bad about 'Marion Miller'?" Ellen asked.

Derrick spoke up right away. "Don't you remember his letter? Marion Miller is a guy."

"Oh," she replied. She knew names like that were a sore point with Derrick.

We planned our first general meeting for July 15th, that weekend, at my place.

Which was kind of a problem. I knew Mom

was still not very happy about things. I knew I couldn't ask her to bake anything for refreshments.

I told her about the meeting. And the letters. She listened. I tried to be honest about everything except for the name of our club.

She thinks it's the I Don't Care For My Name Club. She has a thing about the word hate.

"I'll bring the punch," Ellen said. "I don't have time to cook. I have to help my uncle at his pet shop that afternoon."

I wanted to talk more about Ellen's work with animals, but somehow the conversation was dead set on our club business.

"So who's making refreshments?" Derrick asked. "I placed the ad."

"I mailed twenty-four letters about the meeting so I should be excused from any cooking," Chloe replied.

Everyone looked at me.

"Okay, I'll bake cupcakes or something."

This time Chloe cracked up. "You? You haven't baked anything in your life."

"So, I'll start now. Any fool can read the directions on the back of a box."

"Well," Chloe replied, "since you *are* a fool, you could probably do it."

Everyone laughed.

"Funny," I said.

"Maybe you could get Jennifer to help you. Isn't she coming back tomorrow?" Derrick suggested.

I didn't say anything, but I kind of liked the idea.

It looked like everything was planned for the meeting. Chloe enclosed a map in each letter that she made copies of in the library. Chloe even remembered to include the bus route. Some kids lived far away.

I decided to relax after all the decision-making I had been doing lately, so I laid down on the couch and watched an old Laurel and Hardy movie on television.

That's when Chloe disturbed me.

"What's it like to be in love?"

I sat up and just stared at her. My eyes must have doubled in size. "You're asking ME?"

"Well, I'm writing this novel, *Dorothy's First Kiss* and . . ."

"I thought it was Marsha?" I asked.

"Well, I changed it. She falls in love with a guy named Melvin."

My stomach felt sick. Dorothy and Melvin. Who would ever want to read about them?

"I'm at the point in my novel where I have to describe how it feels to hold someone you love in your arms."

I looked around the living room to see if anyone might be listening. This conversation had the makings of a real disaster. "Not so loud," I said.

"Mom's outside in the garden. Dad won't be home for another hour. It's private."

Ralph jumped on my lap.

"Except for Ralph," she added.

Ralph put his head on my chest and watched Chloe wave her hands as she spoke.

"So . . . I was hoping you could tell me what it's like."

"Me? I've never been in love."

"Yeah? What's this then?" Chloe had a letter in her hand. The name Jennifer Washburn was in the upper left-hand corner. It was postmarked Maine.

"Give that to me!" I shouted.

"I just brought in the afternoon mail. No more Orp letters, but this one looked kind of special." She flashed her peppermint teeth at me again.

"Do you brush your teeth ten times a day or something?"

"I don't like to go to the dentist," Chloe explained. It was true. She was nine and never had a cavity.

"See the heart on it?"

"Where?" I turned the envelope over. There it was. A red heart sticker.

"You must have held her in your arms. What's it like?"

I took the couch pillow and hit Chloe over the head with it. "GET OUT OF HERE, OR I'LL KILL!" I stood up on the couch and tried to look my fiercest.

"Too bad," she said turning around to walk out of the room. "But you missed your chance to be included in great literature."

I doubted *Dorothy's First Kiss* would ever be a classic. No way.

I laid back on the couch and opened Jennifer's letter. Ralph snuggled back on my chest and nuzzled his nose next to the paper.

"You're the only one who can share this with me," I told him.

Sea Winds Motel
BAR HARBOR, MAINE

Dear Orville,

I really had a wonderful time that day in Hartford. Especially on the Ferris wheel. I'll remember that ride always.

We spent a week in Maine. It rained a lot. Dad was glad it wasn't so humid. He slept most of the time. Mom and I took lots of walks along the shore. I found some neat looking rocks for your collection.

One of my favorites is enclosed for you. Do you like it? Give a hug to Ralph for me.

Jennifer

P.S. Have you had your first meeting yet? I hope not. I want to be there.

I found the little rock at the bottom of the envelope. It was worn smooth by the water. Perfectly round, and perfectly flat. I missed Jennifer. It was too bad she would have to go back to her hometown in Ohio next month. She was the only one I knew who called me Orville all the time. I looked at the way she wrote my name in the letter. She put little curlycues on the O and at the end of my name. She made it seem so special.

"ORVIE!"

"Yes, Mom," I said.

She was standing in the living room doorway with garden gloves on. "Are you sure you want to have this I Don't Care For My Name Club meeting in our backyard?"

"Yes. It's all arranged, Mom. There are a lot of people around who don't . . . care for their names. One of the things we'll be talking about is not teasing people with unusual names. That's positive, isn't it?"

Mom nodded. "I planted some rose bushes," she said. And then she left the room.

I reread Jennifer's letter and then I gave Ralph a hug. Things were really looking up. Jennifer was coming home in time for our big meeting on Saturday.

8

Chloe Quits

THAT NIGHT, CHLOE TIPTOED INTO MY bedroom. I was hoping she didn't have any more dumb questions about love.

"Orvie?"

I pretended I was sound asleep.

"Did you tell Mom about the meeting Saturday?"

It sounded like the conversation was a sane one, so I answered her. "Yeah."

"What did she say?"

"She wasn't happy about it."

Chloe sat down on my bed. If I had covers over me, I would have pulled them over my face. But I didn't. It was too hot for covers.

"You know something, Orvie?"

I didn't answer. I didn't want to encourage this conversation.

"I was in the library today doing research."

"Research on your romance novel?" I started to put my pillow over my ears.

"Well, I needed a few more names for characters and you weren't around."

I remembered. I went to the store for Mom.

"So I asked the librarian. She gave me this neat book about names. I thought it was babyish at first because there was a picture of a baby on the cover. But it listed 6,400 names in it."

"Six-thousand four-hundred?" That was hard to believe.

"Yeah, and their origins. The librarian told me to look up "onomatology" in the Oxford Dictionary too. Do you know what that means?"

"'Ona' what?"

"Onomatology."

"No, what is it?"

"The study of names."

"No kidding. There's an 'ology' word for the study of names." I knew about biology, and psychology, and geology.

"And," Chloe continued, "even a magazine called *Names*."

"Really?"

"It's put out by the American Name Society."

"There is an American Name Society?"

"Sure is," Chloe replied.

I just knew two societies—The National Geographic Society, and the American Society for the Prevention of Cruelty to Animals.

"Anyway, this book with 6,400 names tells about the origins. Guess what Orville means?"

"What?" I was really interested now.

"City of gold."

I liked that.

"'Or' means gold and 'ville' means town or city in French. That's what the book said."

I put the pillow behind my head. French. So, that's where my name came from. I liked the idea.

"Chloe is Greek for young," she said. "I think my name is interesting now." And then she added as she stood up, "So, I'm quitting the club."

I jumped out of bed. "QUITTING THE CLUB?"

"Yes. Good night," and she headed for the door.

I ran in front of her and blocked her way. "You can't do that! You're my secretary. Who's going to do all the future mailings?"

Chloe shrugged. "Ask your girlfriend, Jennifer."

That was when I moved out of her way and slammed the door. I knew I would never ask my sister to be in any club again.

Now I was going to have to recruit a secretary. Maybe, just maybe, I *could* get Jennifer to be it temporarily, and I could ask her while we were making cupcakes.

Tomorrow.

9

Baking Cupcakes with Jennifer

SATURDAY MORNING, DAD FINALLY fixed the fan just before the Washburns arrived from Maine.

"It's not difficult at all," he said.

Mom wrinkled her eyebrows. "How come it took you so long then?"

I don't think Dad heard her. He has a way of tuning out people when he doesn't like what they say. "One last screw. Done!" And he stood up and plugged it in.

"What's that noise?" I asked. The fan was working but it sounded like a DC-7 taking off on a runway for Japan.

"Perfect!" Dad said, and he took out his newspaper and read it at the kitchen table.

Mom and I just shook our heads.

Then while Mom went out front to wait for the Washburns, I decided to talk with Dad about the club. It was his day off. Maybe he'd listen.

"Dad?"

"Yeah," he said, turning to the sports page.

"Do you like your name?"

To my surprise Dad put his newspaper down. "My name?"

"Yeah. Orville Rudemeyer Pygenski, Sr.?"

Dad got up and looked in the other room. No one was around but us. "I hate my name."

"You do, Dad? Really?"

"People at the office never spell it right, and when they say my name it sounds more like 'or-ball.'"

"If you don't like your name, how come you gave it to me?"

"That was your mother's doing. She feels the first son should have the father's name. I guess I

73

just went along with her wishes. Sorry, son."

I just smiled. I felt a lot better knowing Dad's real feelings about the issue.

"Well, I started this club, and it's called the I Hate My Name Club, and it's meeting today. Twenty-four people may show up at one P.M."

"Wow! You organized this all yourself?"

I could tell Dad was impressed. He wasn't bothering with his newspaper at all. "Well, I had help." And then I told him about our officers and Chloe's finking out.

"Hmmm, so what's on your agenda for the meeting today?"

"Agenda?"

"What are you planning to do?"

"Well, we're going to explain the rules, collect dues, and have refreshments."

"No main speaker?"

Dad had a point. There wasn't much planned for a two-hour meeting. What were we going to do after we finished eating?

"Well, Orv," Dad said as he sipped some coffee, "I don't want to tell you what to do but whenever I go to a meeting, someone is usually a guest speaker."

"Hmmmm." I was giving it a lot of thought.

"They're here!" Mom called from the porch.

My stomach turned over. I was looking forward to seeing Jennifer, but I didn't like being nervous about it.

As soon as Melvin came in the house, he sat down right in front of the fan. "Great! It's fixed. What's that noise?"

"The fan," Mother said with a groan. Then she and Hilda started talking about Maine and lobsters in butter sauce.

It seemed like a good time to rescue Jennifer. "Want to make cupcakes for our meeting?"

"You want to bake in this hot weather?"

I liked Jennifer's answer. It's something I would have said. But there was no getting out of it. Our treasury was empty. I had to bring refreshments, and the only thing in our cupboard to snack on was Frosted Flakes or cake mix.

"We're having our first meeting today at one P.M."

"Oh good, I didn't miss it then."

I noticed Jennifer had a yellow ribbon in her hair.

And her eyes. They were still that YMCA pool blue.

As soon as we turned on the oven, everyone left the kitchen. Even Ralph. Melvin carried the fan into the living room himself.

"You're going to have to tell me how to do this, Jennifer. I've never made cupcakes before."

"It's easy. The directions are right on the back. Do you have eggs and oil?"

"Sure!" I went to the fridge and took out the carton. Then I went in the pantry and reached up into the top cupboard for some oil.

"Here," I said setting them on the table.

Jennifer broke out laughing. "This is a can of motor oil!"

I shook my head. How could I do such a dumb thing? Being around a girl like Jennifer made me kind of crazy.

I brought out the cooking oil.

"Want to crack two eggs? It's good practice."

I took one and rapped it on the edge of the bowl. Mom did it that way lots of times.

"Perfect!" Jennifer replied. Then I noticed she used her fingers to pick out some shells. I had a feeling Jennifer was a little crazy around me, too. How could I have cracked those eggs perfectly if she had to pick out shells in the bowl?

I decided the timing was great to ask her to be secretary of the club. "Do you type?"

Jennifer shook her head no as she added the egg, oil, and some water to the mix. "I should, though. My handwriting isn't very good."

"I think it is. Thanks for your letter. I read it twice." Then I felt dumb for saying that.

Jennifer didn't say anything. She just kept staring at the batter and stirring.

When she finished, she poured the batter into the cupcake tins. "Want to open the door for me?"

"Sure." And when I did Ralph walked in from the living room.

"No, Orville," Jennifer said laughing, "the oven door. Not the kitchen door."

Now I really felt dumb!

Ralph walked up to Jennifer who was bending over with the cupcake tins and took a sniff. I forgot to tell Jennifer about Ralph's sweet tooth. "Look out!" I said.

But it was too late. Ralph licked some batter right out of the tin.

"Look at that cupcake. It's only one-fourth full."

"Don't worry," Jennifer replied, "the hot temperature will kill any germs. Someone will just get a small cupcake."

That was half-eaten by a dog, I thought. I had to make sure Chloe got that one. I decided to break my silence and ask her to join us for refreshments at the club meeting.

At least it would be some kind of revenge.

After we put the cupcakes in the oven (and I opened the right door), Jennifer and I sat down at the kitchen table and talked.

We talked about rocks, and Maine, and school, and Ohio.

Just then Melvin came into the kitchen. "How long are you cooking on a day like this?"

"Just as soon as the buzzer goes off," Jennifer replied.

Buzzer? Ours hasn't worked in a year. "Quick, you better check on the cupcakes," I said, handing her a checkered hot pad.

"Just in time, Orville," Jennifer said, taking them out of the oven.

I looked at them carefully. Burnt around the edges.

"They look fine to me. Can I sample one?" Melvin asked.

"No, Dad. They're for our meeting today. You can have one then."

"Oh, your I Hate My Name Club," he said.

"You know about it?" I asked.

"Jennifer told me. Can I join too? I hate the name Melvin. When I was a kid they used to say, 'Mel smells.'"

I shook my head. It seemed like everyone except my mom didn't like their name. Maybe it was just something you learned to live with.

After Melvin left, I decided to get to some unfinished business.

"So, would you mind being our club secretary for a while, Jennifer?"

"Sure," she said. "But I'll have to write out the notes."

"Perfect," I said. No typewriter could make Os with curlycues like hers.

10

The First and Last "I Hate My Name Club" Meeting

BY TWELVE-THIRTY P.M., WE TRIED TO
have everything ready. Jennifer put a nice red-
checkered tablecloth on the picnic table.

Ellen was stirring the Kool-Aid with a spatula.
I couldn't find a big spoon. Mom wasn't in the
kitchen. She was outside playing canasta with
Hilda and my dad at a card table right in the
middle of the lawn.

"Aren't you about through with your game?" I asked. I didn't want my parents around when the kids were coming any minute.

"Hold your horses, Orv," my dad said. "I've got the makings of a natural canasta."

"We'll see," Mom said with a sly smile.

Hilda put a two on the deck. "I'm freezing the pack. Let's see what happens now."

I shook my head. I knew it was impossible to get rid of them just yet. I looked over at the hammock where the music from the radio was coming. Melvin was snoring away. Jennifer said he didn't like cards. I really wondered what he liked. Probably eating lobsters in Maine.

And burnt cupcakes.

Derrick came up and patted me on the back. "Well, Pres, are you ready?"

"Not really," I said. "I don't have a program or a guest speaker. What are we going to do for two hours?"

"Take roll, tell them the rules, and then collect dues. Remember, two dollars each." And then Derrick pulled out a cigar box. "This is for the money."

Fine, I thought. Rules and dues. At least it was a beginning.

I looked over at the picnic table again. Jennifer

was putting a gumdrop on each of the cupcakes we had made.

"Where did you get those?"

"In Maine. I forgot about them. They were in my purse. I thought they made the cupcakes look more partyish. What do you think?"

I thought she should have left them in Maine. I didn't know about out-of-state gumdrops. They were probably stale. But I lied. "Sounds great, Jennifer."

Derrick tapped me on the shoulder as he looked up at Melvin. "Hey, we can turn up the music and dance for an hour. That's something to do."

That wasn't a bad idea. At least it was an activity.

And people could get acquainted that way.

"Well, Derrick, you really come up with big ideas. First that ad in the *Courant* and now the entertainment."

Derrick shrugged. "Hey, I got a special deal at the newspaper. Only five seventy-five for twenty words."

"Twenty words?" Chloe was standing behind us with a cupcake. She said she'd come for refreshments and then leave.

I snatched the cupcake out of her hand, and

gave her the small one (that had been half-eaten by Ralph). "Here, you're lucky to get this. You deserted the cause, remember?"

Chloe ignored me. "Did you say twenty words, Derrick?"

"Yeah, why?"

I noticed Chloe was reciting to herself and counting on her fingers."Yup, it's twenty-five."

Ellen and Jennifer joined us. They were interested in the conversation.

"Which five words did you leave out?" Chloe asked.

We all looked at Derrick. What *did* he put in the newspaper?

Just then a man about thirty-five appeared in the yard. "Hello, I'm Rufus Huckaby. Is this the I Hate My Name Club meeting?"

We all stared at Derrick in disbelief.

"You left off the words, 'Kids only eight to twelve'?" I asked.

Derrick shrugged. "Hey, I wanted to save the club some money."

"Thanks," I said, wanting to slug him right there and then. But I couldn't. Rufus Huckaby was still standing by Mom's newly planted rose bushes. "Come on in, Rufus," I said.

Chloe dropped her cupcake on the grass.

Ellen covered her eyes with her hands.

Mom and Dad and Hilda stopped playing cards. Dad got up immediately and came over to shake Rufus's hand. "Welcome to the I Hate My Name Club. I'm Orville Rudemeyer Pygenski."

"Hi, Orp!" Rufus said shaking my dad's hand.

Oh, boy, I thought.

I took Derrick by his shirt collar. "How could you do such a thing. This is supposed to be a club for kids. Not grown-ups."

"They don't like their name either," Derrick said meekly.

When I looked up Dad introduced me to Esmeralda Walsh who looked about fifty-five years old, and Druella Smith who was probably Melvin's age, forty-four.

Melvin was up now. He was talking to Quigley Watson who was about seventy-one years old and Percival Northrup who was thirty-five and Candy Kane who looked thirty-eight.

"They used to call me smelly Melly," Melvin said as he walked them into the backyard.

I thought it was Mel smells. Anyway, I was glad to get some grown-up help.

Chloe tapped me on the shoulder. "You planning to schedule other meetings like this?"

"No way!" I said. "How do I get out of this?"

"Well," Chloe said, "there's my research findings."

I turned and looked at my sister, "Will you be our guest speaker today?"

Chloe beamed. "I always knew I was headed for greatness. Of course. I'll be your guest speaker at this important meeting."

I raced up and received the visitors as they entered the yard. I was glad Dad was doing it with me.

As I looked at the gathering, I guessed that Tyrus String was twenty-eight, Euripides Schwartz looked forty, Phineas Hurdle was around sixty, Norman Borman was thirty-two, and Tangerine Shane was thirty-nine.

It looked like some people brought other people who were unhappy with their names. Several of them I didn't even remember writing to us.

Sally Mander and Ignatius Liverton, the only kids, didn't show. Their mothers probably nixed the idea. They probably said the president was a creep-o.

Derrick whispered in my ear, "What do we do?"

"We carry on like we would if they were kids.

No one knows who's who yet. They are probably waiting for Dad to start the meeting. They think he's Orp."

"You going to set them straight?"

"I have to. But I want to wait until everyone's here."

"Give me a chance to collect dues," Derrick replied.

"Forget it Derrick," I said. "This is our LAST meeting."

Derrick didn't look too disappointed.

I looked around. It was time. Everyone was sitting at the picnic table, the card table, or in lawn chairs, or sitting on the grass sipping punch and meeting new people.

"Ladies and gentlemen," I said loudly. I noticed everyone stopped talking and turned to look at me. "I'd like to welcome you to the first and last I Hate My Name Club meeting. My name is Orp. I'm the president."

Everyone looked shocked, and then sort of chuckled. "Many of you met my dad. He has my same name. This was supposed to be a club for kids from eight to twelve but that was accidently left out of the ad," and then I glared at Derrick. He walked over and sat at the picnic table next to Ralph.

Ralph was probably the only one who wasn't mad at him.

"However . . ." and then I noticed Mom looked worried. I decided not to use the word hate again. I continued, "One thing I discovered is that a lot of people *don't care* for their names. Kids *and* grown-ups."

I was surprised when they clapped.

"Would any of you like to share something about your experiences with an unusual name?"

Hilda Washburn stood up first. Mom was sure surprised. "Having the name Hilda is not easy. I felt like I was forty years old when I was eight. Hilda is the name for an older person."

I agreed. But the name fit her now.

One woman who was quite pretty with dark curly hair stood up to speak. "I always hated my name. It's Candy Kane. My parents thought it was cute since I was born on Christmas day, but I've always felt like I have a cutsey-poo name. And I am very angry that my parents named me Candy."

Esmeralda Walsh spoke next. "My name sounds like one of Cinderella's ugly stepsisters."

"Mine does too," Druella Smith agreed.

"My name constantly embarrasses me. Norman Borman sounds like some kind of a joke."

As I listened to everyone complain about their name, I wondered if Orville was so bad.

I was shocked when Mom stood up. MOM?

So was Dad. He looked at me and shrugged.

"I grew up with the name of Margie. Which is nice, I guess. But then that TV show came on, "My Little Margie," and everyone at school called me Little Margie. I didn't like being compared with a silly, daffy character like that."

When she sat back down, she gave me a smile.

It helped to know so many people had the same experiences. Especially Mom.

Then I noticed Ralph. He was pawing at the cupcake Chloe had dropped on the lawn. I watched him gulp the whole thing down.

Just when Waldo Whimper stood up to talk, I noticed Ralph was choking.

THE OUT-OF-STATE gumdrops! I knew those things were trouble!

I ran over to Ralph.

Jennifer shouted, "Is there a vet in the group? The dog is choking!"

My parents came running over. So did the other grown-ups. Ellen pushed her way through the crowd. "I know something about animals," she said. "I work at a pet shop with my uncle."

Quickly Ellen moved her finger around in

Ralph's throat. I was glad Ralph knew Ellen. He didn't move.

A minute later, Ellen pulled out the gumdrop. It was a black one.

Everyone watched as Ralph jumped up and started barking. Jennifer put her hand over her heart. I threw my arms around him and let him lick my whole face twice.

Everyone clapped.

And cheered and started talking about their pets. No one talked about their name any more. I just stayed with Ralph to make sure he was okay. Dad said he was just fine.

After a good twenty minutes of lots of conversation and laughing, Chloe took the tablecloth off and sat on the picnic table.

"Excuse me ladies and gentlemen, if I may interrupt your conversations for five minutes. I have been asked to be your guest speaker today."

Dad looked over at me and smiled.

Everyone found a seat somewhere, in a lawn chair, on the grass, and listened. A lot of people were smiling. I think that they were impressed with Chloe's manner.

I sat down next to the hammock. The fourteen people who came seemed ready to listen. They were sitting with new friends they had made.

"The past few days I have been studying names, quite by accident really. What I found out was something very interesting. A lot of great people have unusual names.

"Think a minute about these names:

Hannibal Hamlin
Schuyler Colfax
Garret A. Hobart
Alben W. Barkley

"Does anyone know who they are?" she asked.

Derrick and I looked at each other and shrugged. Tyrus String spoke out. "I do. They're vice presidents of the United States."

"Right," Chloe continued, "and they became great leaders in spite of their unusual names."

Mom smiled. She liked Chloe's speech.

"Think of these two baseball Hall of Fame players—Tyrus Cobb and Aloysius Simmons. Or that great baseball manager who won five world championships—Cornelius McGillicuddy Mack.

"Englebert Humperdink said his name helped him sell records.

"And consider the poet Waldo Emerson or a

president of Yale University, Kingman Brewster. Certainly these are unusual names too."

And then she cleared her throat. "I would like to end my speech with a quote from *Romeo and Juliet*."

I started to cringe. Here comes the romance.

"A rose by any other name would smell as sweet," and then she pointed to Mom's new rose bushes in the garden.

Candy Kane stood up. "She deserves a standing ovation!"

"I agree," Norman Borman said.

And everyone got up and clapped. My parents did too. Ralph barked.

"What does she mean?" Derrick whispered to me as everyone was clapping. "We should be more like rose bushes?"

For being so smart about money, I expected more from Derrick. "Derrick, when Shakespeare wrote those words he meant it doesn't matter what our names are. We are what we are. If we change our names we're still the same people."

"So," Chloe added, as she held her hand up to stop the applause, "be more concerned with your lives than the sound of your name."

"Bravo!" shouted Esmeralda Walsh.

Ellen petted Ralph. "I'm just glad he's okay. That choking business reminded me about what's really important."

"Me too," I said.

People seemed to be looking around for something to do, so I turned up the radio. "Why don't we all dance for a while," I shouted.

Dad looked at me. "You throw a great party, son. Let's dance Little Margie," he said as he grabbed Mom.

Mom punched him in the shoulder, and then they started doing the box step to a fast tune.

I noticed Norman Borman asked Candy Kane to dance. And Phineas Hurdle asked Esmeralda Walsh.

Melvin went back to his hammock. I guess he didn't like dancing either.

Jennifer came over to me. "Want to dance?" she said.

I looked around. She meant me all right. The only other guy around was Ralph.

"I don't know how, really," I said.

"It's as easy as baking cupcakes," she smiled. And then she started swaying back and forth. I did too.

The first and last I Hate My Name Club meeting turned out not to be so bad after all.

11

Two Months Later

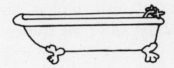

SOMETIMES I THINK ABOUT THAT FIRST and last I Hate My Name Club meeting, and wish we could have met again. There were a lot of interesting people. Different ages, true. But very interesting.

Jennifer writes often. I write back—believe it or not! I know I still hate writing, but it's not a chore when I write to Jennifer. I even enjoy it.

We exchange rocks, and most recently, stamps. Yesterday she sent me one from Australia.

It was news to me that Norman Borman and Candy Kane were engaged. Chloe saw it in the *Hartford Courant.*

Candy wouldn't have to worry about the sound of her name any more. She was going to be Candy Borman.

Mom said she read that Druella Smith and Esmeralda Walsh were bridge partners now. They came in first and their names were in the paper.

Chloe has a new project. She dumped the romance novel.

Hallelujah!

She's doing historical fiction. She's writing a novel about a woman who becomes the first president of the United States. Her name is Hortense McGillicuddy. Chloe doesn't use a pen name any more. She says hers is more distinctive—Chloe Urath Rudemeyer Pygenski.

Me?

Mrs. Lewis is happy with my new project idea. It's onomatology.

And to think all this started in the bathtub!

I better return to my think tank now. I have to be where my ideas flow.